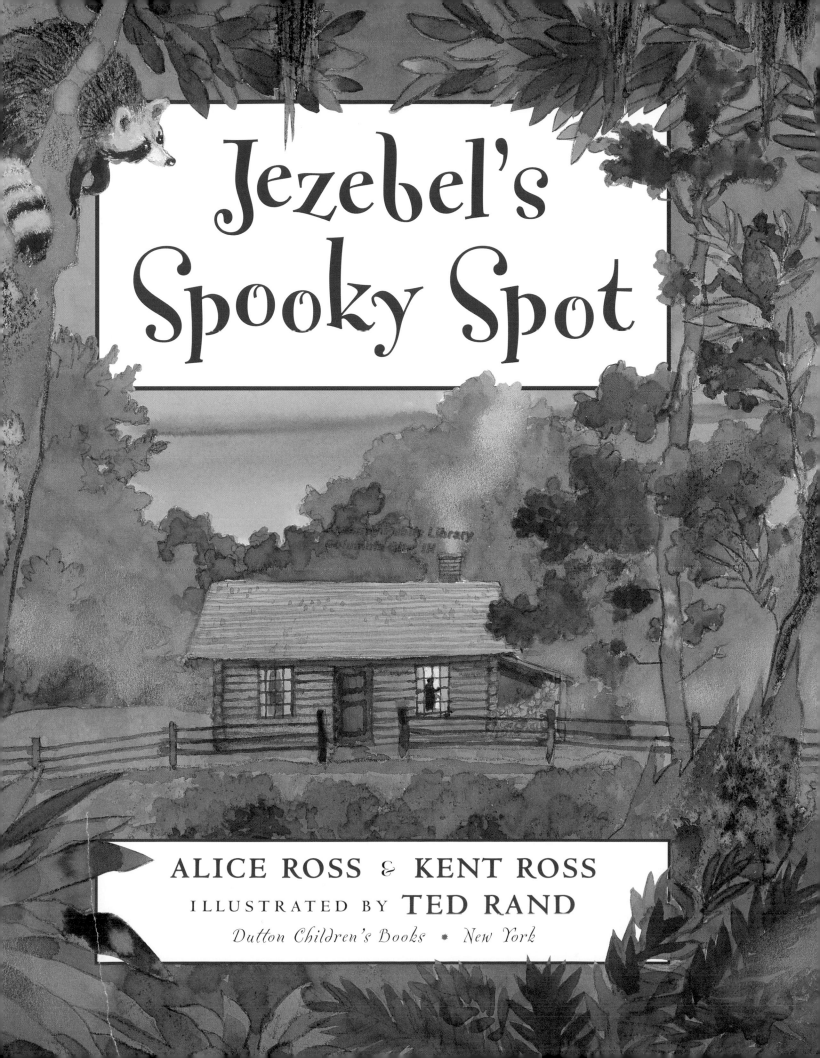

Jezebel's Spooky Spot

ALICE ROSS & KENT ROSS

ILLUSTRATED BY **TED RAND**

Dutton Children's Books ✳ *New York*

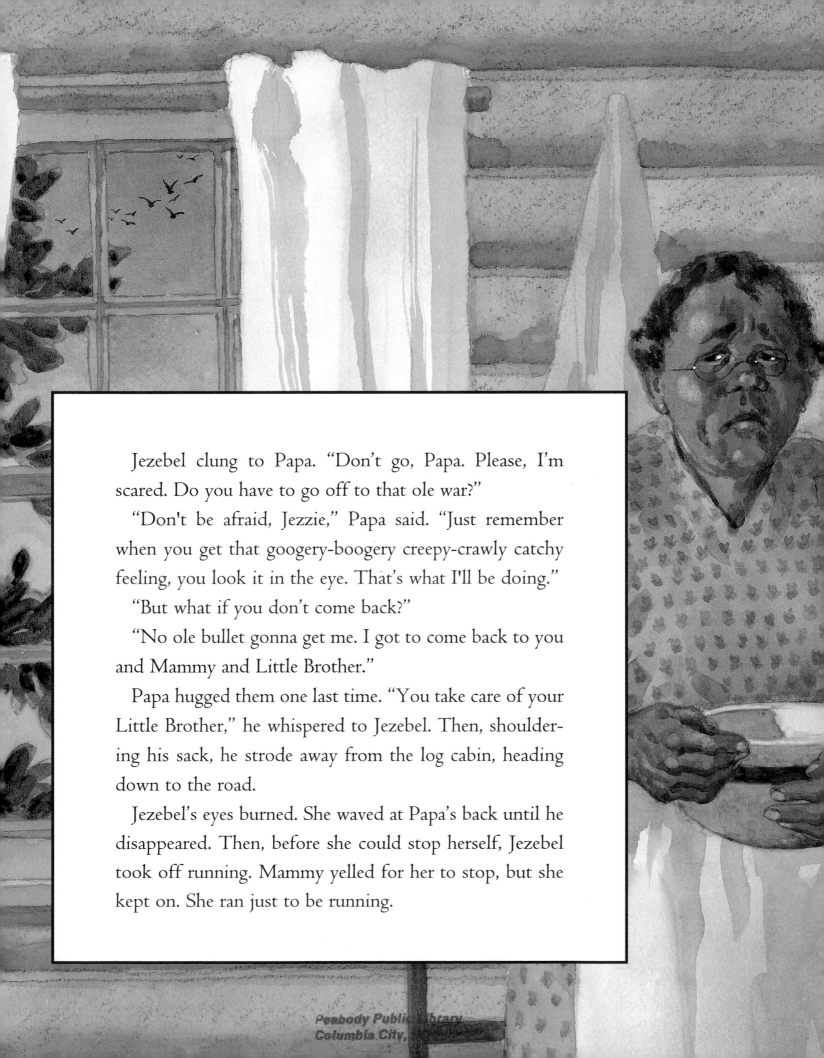

Jezebel clung to Papa. "Don't go, Papa. Please, I'm scared. Do you have to go off to that ole war?"

"Don't be afraid, Jezzie," Papa said. "Just remember when you get that googery-boogery creepy-crawly catchy feeling, you look it in the eye. That's what I'll be doing."

"But what if you don't come back?"

"No ole bullet gonna get me. I got to come back to you and Mammy and Little Brother."

Papa hugged them one last time. "You take care of your Little Brother," he whispered to Jezebel. Then, shouldering his sack, he strode away from the log cabin, heading down to the road.

Jezebel's eyes burned. She waved at Papa's back until he disappeared. Then, before she could stop herself, Jezebel took off running. Mammy yelled for her to stop, but she kept on. She ran just to be running.

Deep into the woods she stumbled, into the marsh where woolly cypress trees sank their fat feet into dark, mushy soil. Oh, it was moky! Brambly bushes nibbled her knees and tried to scramble up under her shirt to scratch her belly. A thornbush snapped at her leg, and she jerked away, tripping on a root, falling over a hump of ground covered with rotten leaves and moss.

Jezebel lay still, her heart pounding the earth. Tears stung her cheeks, and musty-smelling moss prickled her neck.

When her tears dried, she looked around in the leaf-light. A small clearing that overlooked a pool of tar-colored water held her. A crowd of weeping trees nearby reached out gnarled, twisted, two-fingered hands trying to poke a real, blood-and-flesh girl. Tall weeds sang with a breeze, "Don't 'sturb this spooky spot. This is ooouuurrr spot."

"Papa, I'm scared," Jezebel whispered. When she said the words, that googery-boogery creepy-crawly catchy feeling Papa talked about came on her.

Then a light caught her eye. Man in the moon was casting down through the willows, smiling at her. Seeing that smile, she felt a little better. Papa had told her not to be afraid, and she wouldn't be.

Jezebel stood up and dusted off. "No spot in these woods gonna scare me," she declared. "I'm stubborn enough, you ole spooky spot, to spite you." She shook her fist at the trees and snaky weeds that leaned close. "It's not your spot anymore. It's mine," she told them. And as she spoke, her fear got up and cleared out.

"And I'll be back whenever I feel like it. This be *my* spot now."

Stirring Little Brother's mush for breakfast the next morning, Jezebel said to him, "I found a spooky spot yesterday."

Mammy looked up from poking the fire. "Lawse, girl, I told you to stay away from them woods. Wicked things be in there."

Jezebel thought about the wicked things she knew. "It's not wicked as Mama dying. Not wicked as Papa going off to war," she said.

Little Brother was curious. "Did you run away fast?"

"Not me," said Jezebel, plopping a spoonful of mush in his dish. "No scary spot gonna spook me!"

In a few weeks, a long lonely time came on Jezebel. She missed Papa so bad. When she finished hauling water, she headed off to find that spot in the marsh. Mammy had said it was a dangerous place. But it made Jezebel feel close to Papa, because he was in danger, too.

The woods didn't seem so spooky this time. She wandered down two false tracks until she glimpsed the hump between the trees. When she got there, she clambered up and WHAM! She ducked smack into the thick, sticky web of Mister Spider. In her hair, in her eyes, on her arms, the web wrapped its ropes around her. Jezebel pulled back, shivering, searching for Mister Spider. Mammy always said his poison could rot you alive!

There he be! Bouncing down his ropes, coming at her, wanting to bite her.

Jezebel felt that googery-boogery creepy-crawly catchy feeling shimmy over her. "Oh, Papa," she cried. "I gotta run."

But she didn't. Thinking about Papa made that stubborn streak rise up in her.

"Set your trap another place, Mister Spider. This be *my* spot." She pulled tickly, sticky stuff off her nose and out of her hair, and scrubbed at her arms and legs. Mister Spider just took off into the weeds, running from his wrecked home, in a hurry to build another one.

When Jezebel got back to the cabin, Little Brother squinted up at her. "You been to the woods again, Sister? What you see this time?"

"Mister Spider tried to wrap me up and eat me alive!"

Mammy shook her spoon at Jezebel. "Why you want to go in them woods, child? You get spider-bit, and you won't see me nursing you."

"Were you scared?" asked Little Brother.

Jezebel gave him a wink. "Spider likes a big fat fly, not a skinny little girl."

One cold morning before light, when ice filled the chinks of the cabin walls, that low, lonely feeling woke Jezebel. What was Papa doing? Was he lonely, too? Were his hands as cold as hers? She got up from her mat and pulled on Papa's old boots, then she wrapped her hands in rags and snuck out of the cabin.

Dawn light danced off the icy leaves as she walked. She had to leap puddles of frozen mud, but she found her spot all right. As she stood on the hump, sucking in the cold air, fog fingers rose from the steaming pool. Slowly, they transformed into wispy man-shapes floating between the trees.

Swamp ghosts!

The ghosts gathered closer and closer, crowding around, hemming her in.

That googery-boogery creepy-crawly catchy feeling slid over Jezebel's arms. Her teeth bucked and bounced with fear, and her legs twitched to run away.

She thought of Papa running through the smoke and mist and dirt thrown up from bullets and shells. "I gotta stay strong for Mammy and Little Brother," she said. "I won't give in. Now you get away, ghosts! This be *my* place!"

Then a flash of bright morning sun winked across the water, and the fog ghosts began to melt. They settled softly, curling round Jezebel, nestling her safely, like a baby in a cotton blanket.

When Little Brother saw Jezebel walking out of the woods, he called, "Did something try to git you?"

"Just some ghosts walking on the water, coming to drag me to the bottom of the pool."

"What happened?"

"Them ghosts drew way back when they saw Miss Jezebel was not gonna skedaddle from *her* spot."

Summer limped in, and Jezebel was nearly worn out doing all Papa's hoeing and picking and shelling. Her back was yelling at her with pain, and her hands were scabbed from blisters. Papa had been gone so long . . . but Jezebel never gave up hope. It was just that sometimes the loneliness nearly swamped her.

One evening, after a hot day in the garden, she slipped down to her spooky spot. She stayed late, and the darkness gathered around her. Suddenly, pixie lights flickered and flashed among the cane.

A powerful deep-down googery-boogery creepy-crawly catchy feeling swarmed over Jezebel. Mammy always said pixie lights could steal your soul.

She had to get away. She took off running.

But the pixie lights chased her, whizzing past, humming by her ears like bullets in the war.

"Run, Papa," she shouted. "Don't let them kill you. Run!"

She tripped over the knee of a cypress tree, flopping straight onto her belly.

Overhead the lights still flashed.

Then she knew.

Papa would never run. He might be afraid, but he would never run.

Jezebel jumped up and faced the swooping lights. "We're not afraid!" she cried. The lights drew in, circling her, diving and dancing. She put out her hand, and one landed on her finger. She watched it blink on and off. Then it flew away, leaving behind a soft glow.

Later, Jezebel showed Mammy and Little Brother the pixie fire on her finger.

"Lawse a mercy, that pixie fire will steal your soul," Mammy said.

"Not mine," said Jezebel. And she popped the glowing finger into her mouth and licked the pixie fire, just like it was honey.

Little Brother laughed.

Fall drifted in, and still there was no word from Papa. Where was he? Was he hurt? Was he dead?

Jezebel had not been to her spot in a long time, but today she needed to go, even though there was work to be done.

The leaves crinkled and crackled on the path, so a body got scared just walking. Jezebel found the place easily and climbed up. Her spot was unusually still, the quiet broken only by the cricking of a frog.

Oh, Papa, you can't be dead, she thought. *You just can't be.*

Then, thinking such a scary thought, she got a touch of that googery-boogery creepy-crawly catchy feeling.

Suddenly the frog hushed. She leaned forward, listening. A noise. She heard twigs snapping. The noise was moving closer, crunching louder and louder.

Something big was coming. Something as big as a bear was stomping and stamping through the leaves.

Her heart heaved out of her chest, and that googery-boogery creepy-crawly catchy feeling clamped down mightily. It tingled her neck, skittered down her arms, and buzzed clean to her toes.

Jezebel turned to run, but something grabbed her from behind. It lifted her off the ground! Jezebel kicked and slugged, hollering like a panther cat. But it clung tighter, crushing the air out of her. Jezebel elbowed and kicked.

"Ow, ow," said the creature. "Sakes alive, you growed up. Always were a stubborn, mule-headed wildcat. Stop, Jezzie, stop!"

When Jezebel heard her nickname, she froze. Only Papa called her Jezzie. Twisting around, she looked up through the fading light into the eyes of her papa.

"Oh, Papa, Papa, you near scared me to death!" She held tight to keep from shaking.

He smiled. "I'm just trying to hug my girl."

She touched the bandage on his head. "Papa, you're hurt."

"Ole bullet come my way. But I tell him, 'Get outta here. I'm going back home. Jezzie and Little Brother need me.'

"So," he added, setting her on the ground in front of him, "I see you found my special spot."

"*Your* spot, Papa?"

"Sure, I always come here in the lonely times. It's a good place for figuring things out. I reckoned you might be using it, too."

Jezebel shook her head in wonder. "So now it'll be *our* spot?"

"Sure, Jezzie. It'll be our spot now."

As they turned and headed for the yellow light of the cabin, Jezebel wondered if things would really be all right now. She caught a twinge of that googery-boogery creepy-crawly catchy feeling coming over her again.

But when she looked up at Papa's face, she felt the old feeling leaking out, seeping out the bottom of her bare feet.

Seeping all the way out.

Till it was plum gone.

To Chapin, dedicated husband and father

A.R.
K.R.

Text copyright © 1999 by Alice Ross and Kent Ross
Illustrations copyright © 1999 by Ted Rand

Library of Congress Cataloging-in-Publication Data

Ross, Alice.
Jezebel's Spooky Spot / by Alice Ross and Kent Ross; illustrated by Ted Rand.—Ist ed. p. cm.
"A read-aloud picture/story book."
Summary: When Jezebel's papa goes to war, she finds a special place in the woods to do battle with her own fears.
ISBN 0-525-45448-9 (hc)
[I. Separation anxiety—Fiction. 2. Fear—Fiction. 3. Fathers and daughters—Fiction.] I. Ross, Kent. II. Rand, Ted, ill. III. Title.
PZ7.R719694Jf 1998 [Fic]—dc2I 97-32707 CIP AC

Published in the United States 1999 by Dutton Children's Books, a division of Penguin Putnam Books for Young Readers
345 Hudson Street, New York, New York I0014 • Designed by Ellen M. Lucaire
Printed in Hong Kong • First Edition
I 3 5 7 9 10 8 6 4 2